TECK-VAUGHN ✪ BOLDPRINT kids

MW00932498

FOOD FOR THOUGHT

Gwen McCutcheon
Art by Gavin McCarthy

GRAPHIC READERS

Literacy Consultants
David Booth • Larry Swartz

Ru'bicon www.rubiconpublishing.com

Editorial Director: Amy Land
Project Editor: Dawna McKinnon
Creative Director: Jennifer Drew
Art Director: Rebecca Buchanan

Printed in Singapore

ISBN: 978-1-77058-558-4
3 4 5 6 7 8 9 10 11 12   2016   25 24 23 22 21 20 19 18 17 16
4500568921

Who will rule the veggie bin?

CHARACTERS

Bananas

Pea Pods

Cucumbers

Green Beans

Red Pepper

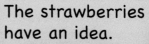

The cucumbers are first in the competition.

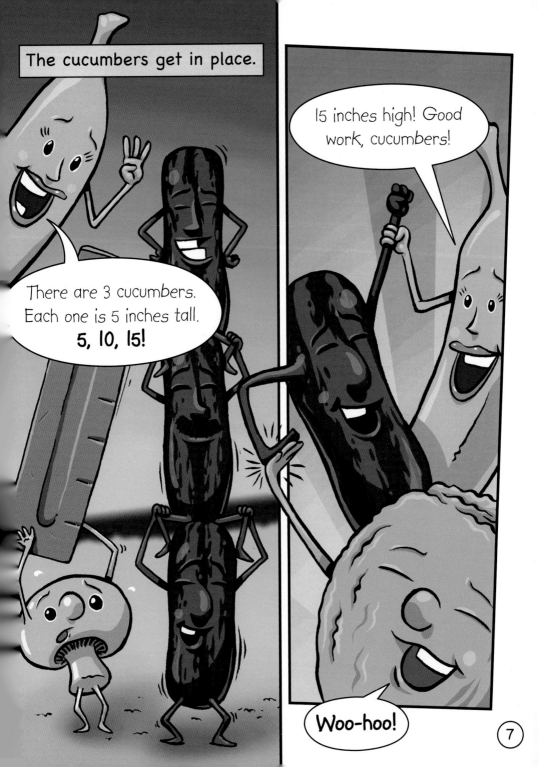

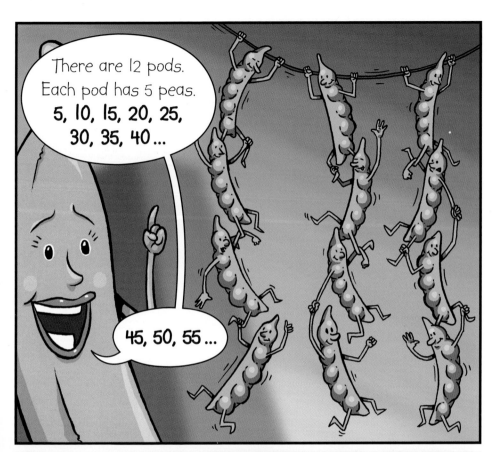

11

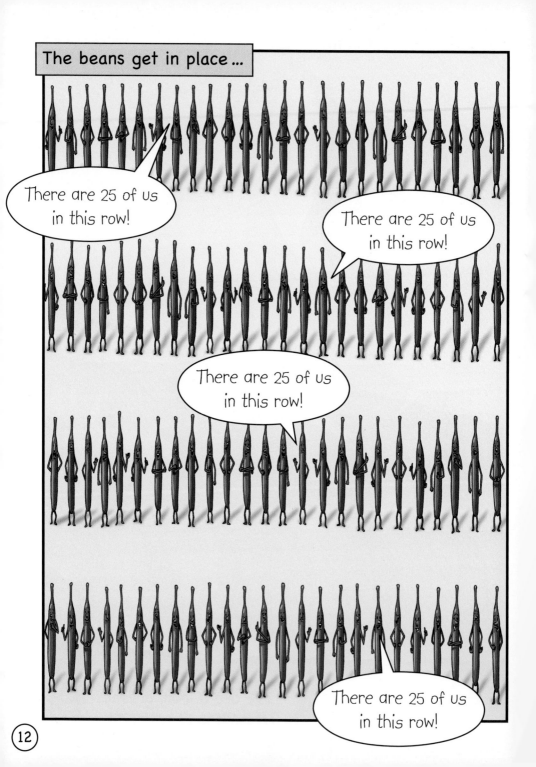

The veggies begin to celebrate!

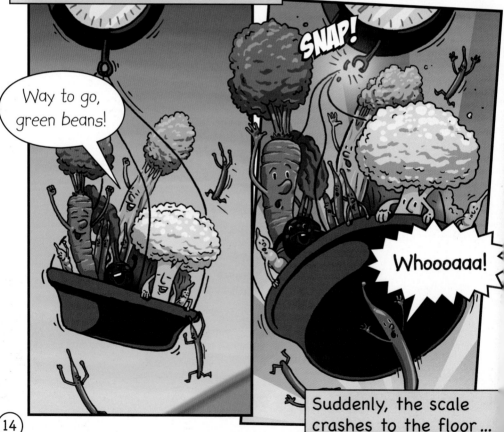

Comprehension Strategy: Asking Questions

Common Core Reading Standards

Foundational Skills
3e. Identify words with inconsistent but common spelling-sound correspondences.

Informational Text
1. Ask and answer such questions as *who, what, where, when, why,* and *how* to demonstrate understanding
3. Describe the connection between a series of historical events, scientific ideas or concepts, or steps in technical procedures in a text.
5. Know and use various text features
7. Explain how specific images (e.g., a diagram showing how a machine works) contribute to and clarify a text.
10. By the end of the year, read and comprehend informational texts

Reading Foundations
Word Study: Multiple Meaning Words
High-Frequency Words: anything, dark, each, first, learn, next, night, number, place, really, sounds, store, win
Reading Vocabulary: beat, celebrate, challenge, compete, competition, fruits, grocery, pepper, rule, team, vegetable
Fluency: Stressing Words with Special Type

BEFORE Reading

Prereading Strategy Activating Prior Knowledge

- Introduce the book by reading the title aloud. Point to the vegetables on the cover. Say: *We know that vegetables keep us strong and healthy. Let's make a text-to-self connection. What are your favorite vegetables?*

Introduce the Comprehension Strategy

- Point to the Asking Questions visual on the inside front cover of this book. Say: *Today we will practice asking questions about the text. Asking questions such as* who, what, where, when, why, *and* how *as you read helps you make sure you understand the text. Let's review question words.*
- Draw a hand on the board. Label the fingers with the five *W*s and the palm with *How*? Review each word. Turn to page 3. Model how to ask questions.
  Modeling Example Say: *As I look at page 3, a few questions come to mind. I don't recognize all the vegetables on the cover. What are they? Why is the red vegetable yelling? Why is the strawberry cheering?* Draw a T-chart on the board labeled *My Questions* and *Answers*, and write your questions in the first column. Say: *As I read, I'll look for answers to these questions. As I find them, I'll write the answers in the* Answers *column.*
- Remind children to ask who, what, where, when, why, and how as they read.